Marx Machiavelli Chesterton Emerson Joyce
Abbott Hardy Montaigne Cooper Austen
Defoe Melville Haggard Hugo
Carroll Christie Eliot Grimm
Stoker Molière
Wilde Maupassant Byron
Engels Schiller
Garnett Einstein Fitzgerald Hawthorne Smith Kafka
Goethe Dostoyevsky
Cotton Kipling Doyle Hall
Baum Leslie Dumas Henry Willis
Nietzsche
Flaubert Turgenev Balzac
Stockton Vatsyayana Crane
Burroughs Verne
Curtis Tocqueville Whitman Gogol Vinci
Homer Widger Tolstoy Busch
Darwin Thoreau
Potter Freud Zola Twain Plato Scott
Lawrence
Kant Jowett Stevenson Dickens
Andersen Burton Hesse Harte
London Descartes Cervantes
Poe Aristotle Wells Voltaire
Hale James Hastings
Bunner Shakespeare Cooke
Richter Chambers Irving
Doré Swift Dante Chekhov da Shaw Wodehouse Benedict Alcott
Pushkin
Newton

tredition

tredition was established in 2006 by Sandra Latusseck and Soenke Schulz. Based in Hamburg, Germany, tredition offers publishing solutions to authors and publishing houses, combined with worldwide distribution of printed and digital book content. tredition is uniquely positioned to enable authors and publishing houses to create books on their own terms and without conventional manufacturing risks.

For more information please visit: www.tredition.com

TREDITION CLASSICS

This book is part of the TREDITION CLASSICS series. The creators of this series are united by passion for literature and driven by the intention of making all public domain books available in printed format again - worldwide. Most TREDITION CLASSICS titles have been out of print and off the bookstore shelves for decades. At tredition we believe that a great book never goes out of style and that its value is eternal. Several mostly non-profit literature projects provide content to tredition. To support their good work, tredition donates a portion of the proceeds from each sold copy. As a reader of a TREDITION CLASSICS book, you support our mission to save many of the amazing works of world literature from oblivion. See all available books at www.tredition.com.

Project Gutenberg

The content for this book has been graciously provided by Project Gutenberg. Project Gutenberg is a non-profit organization founded by Michael Hart in 1971 at the University of Illinois. The mission of Project Gutenberg is simple: To encourage the creation and distribution of eBooks. Project Gutenberg is the first and largest collection of public domain eBooks.

Child Songs of Cheer

Evaleen Stein

Imprint

This book is part of TREDITION CLASSICS

Author: Evaleen Stein
Cover design: Buchgut, Berlin – Germany

Publisher: tredition GmbH, Hamburg - Germany
ISBN: 978-3-8472-2897-4

www.tredition.com
www.tredition.de

The intention of the TREDITION CLASSICS series is to make world literature in the public domain available in printed format. Literary enthusiasts and organizations, such as Project Gutenberg, worldwide have scanned and digitally edited the original texts. tredition has subsequently formatted and redesigned the content into a modern reading layout. Therefore, we cannot guarantee the exact reproduction of the original format of a particular historic edition. Please also note that no modifications have been made to the spelling, therefore it may differ from the orthography used today.

DANDELIONS

Dandelions, dandelions, shining through the dew,
Let the Kings have Cloth of Gold, but let *us* have *you*!

CHILD SONGS OF CHEER

BY

EVALEEN STEIN

ILLUSTRATIONS BY
ANTOINETTE INGLIS

BOSTON
LOTHROP, LEE & SHEPARD CO.

ILLUSTRATIONS BY

ANTOINETTE INGLIS

Dear Children, all the little words
These printed pages through,
They are a flock of little birds
I bring to sing to you.

Sometimes they sing of foolish things,
And other times they try
To tell their gladness when their wings
Soar up to seek the sky.

So, Sweethearts, do but kindly hark!
If but a sparrow throng,
Or if among them there's a lark,
To you their songs belong!

Contents

Illustrations

Child Songs of Cheer

[11]

UP, LITTLE ONES!

A robin redbreast, fluting there
Upon the apple-bough,
Is telling all the world how fair
Are apple-blossoms now;
The honey-dew its sweetness spills
From cuckoo-cups, and all
The crocuses and daffodils
Are drest for festival!

Such pretty things are to be seen,
Such pleasant things to do,
The April earth it is so green,
The April sky so blue,
[12] The path from dawn to even-song
So joyous is to-day,
Up, little ones! and dance along
The lilac-scented way!

[13]

DANDELIONS

Hey-a-day-a-day, my dear! Dandelion time!
Come, and let us make for them a pretty little rhyme!

See the meadows twinkling now, beautiful and bright
As the sky when through the blue shine the stars at night!

Once upon a time, folks say, mighty kings of old
Met upon a splendid field called "The Cloth of Gold."

But, we wonder, could it be there was ever seen
Brighter gold than glitters now in our meadows green?
[14]
Dandelions, dandelions, shining through the dew,
Let the kings have Cloth of Gold, but let *us* have *you*!

[15]

OUR PUPPIES

Little ears as soft as silk,
Little teeth as white as milk,
Little noses cool and pink,
Little eyes that blink and blink,
Little bodies round and fat,
Little hearts that pit-a-pat,
Surely prettier puppies never
Were before nor can be ever!

[16]

THE LOST BALLOON

O dear! my purple toy balloon
Has flown away! and very soon
It will be high up as the moon!

And don't you think the man up there
Will wonder what it is, and stare?
Perhaps hell say, "*Well, I declare!*"

Or, maybe if it chance there are
Some little boys in yonder star,
And if it floats away so far,

Perhaps they'll jump up very high
And catch the cord as it goes by!
At any rate I hope they'll try!

[17]

THE CIRCUS PROCESSION

Oh, hurry! hurry! here they come,
The band in front with the big bass drum
And blaring bugles,—there they are,
On golden thrones in a golden car,
Tooting and fluting, oh, how grand!
Hi diddle, diddle!
The fife and the fiddle!
Hurrah, hurrah for the circus band!

And the red-plumed horses, oh, see them prance
And daintily lift their hoofs and dance,
While beautiful ladies with golden curls
Are jingling their bridles of gold and pearls,
And close behind
Come every kind
Of animal cages great and small,
O how I wonder what's in them all!
[18]
Here's one that's open and glaring there
Is the shaggiest snow-white polar bear!
Woof! but I wonder what we'd do
If his bars broke loose right now, don't you?
And O dear me!
Just look and see
That pink-cheeked lady in skirts of gauze
And the great big lion with folded paws!
O me! O my!
I'm glad that I
Am not in that lion's cage, because

Suppose he'd open his horrible jaws!
—But look! the clown is coming! Of course
Facing the tail of a spotted horse
And shouting out things to make folks laugh,
And grinning up at the tall giraffe
That placidly paces along and looks
Just like giraffes in the picture-books!
[19]
And there are the elephants, two and two,
Lumbering on as they always do!
The men who lead them look so small
I wonder the elephants mind at all
As they wag their queer
Long trunks, and peer
Through their beady eyes,—folks say they know
No end of things, and I'm sure it's so!
And you never must do a thing that's bad
Or that possibly might make an elephant mad,
For he'll never forgive you, it appears,
And will punish you sure, if it takes him *years!*
So do not stare
But take good care
To mind your manners, and always try
To smile politely as they go by!
[20]
But the camels don't care if you laugh at them
With their bumpy humps like a capital M,
They lurch and sway
And seem to say,
As they wrinkle their noses, long and gray,
"This swaggering stride is quite the plan,
It's the way we walked in the caravan!"

And now more cages come rumbling by
With glittering people throned on high;
So many spangles and precious things,
They surely must all be queens and kings!
They look so proud
Above the crowd,

O my, how fine it must feel to ride
On golden wagons that hide inside
Strange animals caught in cannibal isles
And brought in ships for a million miles!
[21] But hark! it's near
The end, for hear
That sudden screeching in piercing key!
The steaming, screaming *cal-li-o-pe*!
Just plain pianos sound terribly tame
Beside this one with the wonderful name,
And wouldn't you love some day to sit
In a circus wagon and play on it?

[22]

MAY-BASKETS

Let us take our baskets early
To the meadows green,
While the wild-flowers still are pearly
With the dewdrops' sheen.

Fill them full of blossoms rosy,
Violets and gay
Cowslips, every pretty posy
Welcoming the May.

Then our lovely loads we'll carry
Down the village street,
On each door, with laughter merry,
Hang a basket sweet.

Hey-a-day-day! It is spring now,
Lazy folks, awake!
See the pretty things we bring now
For the May-day's sake!

[23]

THE PICTURE-BOOK GIANT

Once there was a fierce, defiant,
Greedy, grumpy, grizzly giant
In the pages of a picture-book, and he
Sometimes screamed, in sudden rages,
"I must jump out from these pages,
For this life's a much too humdrum one for me!
Fiddle-dee!
Yes, this life's a quite too quiet one for me!"

So one rainy day he did it,
Took the picture-book and hid it,
Stamped his foot, and shouting loudly,
"Now I'm free!"
Boldly started out, forgetting
That he could not stand a wetting!
[24] He was just a paper giant, don't you see?
Dearie me!
Just a gaudy, picture giant, don't you see?

[25]

DID YOU EVER?

Did you ever see a fairy in a rose-leaf coat and cap
Swinging in a cobweb hammock as he napped his noonday nap?

Did you ever see one waken very thirsty and drink up
All the honey-dew that glimmered in a golden buttercup?

Did you ever see one fly away on rainbow-twinkling wings?
If you did not, why, how comes it that you never see such things?

[26]

DECORATION DAY

See the soldiers, little ones!
Hark the drummers' beat!
See them with their flags and guns
Marching down the street!

Tattered flags from out the wars,
Let us follow these
To the little stripes and stars
Twinkling through the trees.

Watch them waving through the grass
Where the heroes sleep!
Thither gently let us pass
On this day we keep.

Let us bring our blossoms, too,
All our gardens grow;
Lilacs honey-sweet with dew,
And the lilies' snow.
[27]
Every posy of the May,
Every bloomy stem,
Every bud that breaks to-day
Gather now for them.

Lay the lilies o'er them thus,
Lovingly, for so
Down they laid their lives for us,
Long and long ago.

Heap above them bud and bough;
Softly, ere we cease,
God, we pray Thee, gently now
Fold them in Thy peace!

[28]

CHU-CHU CARS

Turn the chairs down in a row
Each behind the other, so;
Chu-chu! Chu-chu! there they are,
Passenger and baggage-car,
Chu-chu-chu! the Morris chair
Is the engine puffing there,
Chu-chu! Chu-chu! Ting-a-ling!
Don't you hear its big bell ring?
All aboard! Jump on! if you
Want to take this train. *Chu-chu!!*
Off we start now, rushing fast
Through the fields and valleys, past
Noisy cities, over bridges,
Hills and plains and mountain ridges,
Chu-chu! Chu-chu! Chu-chu-chu!!
At such speed it must be true
[29] Since we started we have come
Most a million miles from home!
Jump off, some one! Quick! and go
To the pantry, for, you know,
We must have the cookie-jar
For our Pullman dining-car!

[30]

FAIRY RINGS

Softly in the gloaming
Flitting through the vale,
Fairy folk are roaming
Over hill and dale.

Pixies in the hollow,
Elves upon the height,

Let us follow, follow
Through the paling light.

Follow, all unbidden,
To the grassy glade
Wrapped around and hidden
In the forest shade.

Hark the elfin tinkle
Of their little lutes!
Mark the golden twinkle
Of their fairy flutes!

FAIRY RINGS

[31]

See them dancing, dancing,
While the silver moon
Tips their swiftly glancing
Little silver shoon!

Tripping, tripping lightly,
Where their footprints fall,
Look! the grass is brightly
Growing green and tall!

Springing close, unbroken,
In a fairy ring,
For to-morrow's token
Of their frolicking!

[32]

THE FIREFLY

Flash and flicker and fly away,
Trailing light as you flutter far,
Are you a lamp for the fairies, say?
Or a flake of fire from a falling star?

[33]

A RAIN SONG

Tinkle, tinkle,
Lightly fall
On the peach buds, pink and small;
Tip the tiny grass, and twinkle
On the clover, green and tall.

Tinkle, tinkle,—
Faster now,

Little rain-drops, smite and sprinkle
Cherry-bloom and apple-bough!
Pelt the elms, and show them how
You can dash!
And splash! splash! splash!
While the thunder rolls and mutters,
And the lightnings flash and flash!
[34] Then eddy into curls
Of a million misty swirls,
And thread the air with silver, and embroider it with pearls!

And patter, patter, patter
To a quicker time, and clatter
On the streaming window-pane;
Rain, rain,
On the leaves,
And the eaves,
And the turning weather-vane!

Rush in torrents from the tip
Of the gable-peak, and drip
In the garden-bed, and fill
All the cuckoo-cups, and pour
More and more
[35] In the tulip-bowls, and still
Overspill
In a crystal tide until
Every yellow daffodil
Is flooded to its golden rim, and brimming o'er and o'er!

Then as gently as the low
Muffled whir of robin wings,
Or a sweep of silver strings,
Even so,
Take your airy April flight
Through the merry April light,
And melt into a mist of rainy music as you go!

[36]

FAIRIES

Grandfather says that sometimes,
When stars are twinkling and
A new moon shines, there come times
When folks see fairy-land!

So when there's next a new moon,
I mean to watch all night!
Grandfather says a blue moon
Is best for fairy light,

And in a peach-bloom, maybe,
If I look I shall see
A little fairy baby
No bigger than a bee!

[37]

THE LITTLE FIR-TREES

Hey! little evergreens,
Sturdy and strong!
Summer and autumn time
Hasten along;
Harvest the sunbeams, then,
Bind them in sheaves,
Range them, and change them
To tufts of green leaves.
Delve in the mellow mold,
Far, far below,
And so,
Little evergreens, grow!
Grow, grow!
Grow, little evergreens, grow!
[38]

Up, up so airily
To the blue sky,
Lift up your leafy tips
Stately and high;
Clasp tight your tiny cones,
Tawny and brown;
By and by, buffeting
Rains will pelt down;
By and by, bitterly
Chill winds will blow;
And so,
Little evergreens, grow!
Grow, grow!
Grow, little evergreens, grow!

Gather all uttermost
Beauty, because,—
Hark, till I tell it now!
How Santa Claus,
[39] Out of the northern land,
Over the seas,
Soon shall come seeking you,
Evergreen trees!
Seek you with reindeer soon,
Over the snow;
And so,
Little evergreens, grow!
Grow, grow!
Grow, little evergreens, grow!

What if the maples flare
Flaunting and red,
You shall wear waxen white
Tapers instead!
What if now, otherwhere,
Birds are beguiled,
You shall yet nestle
The little Christ-child!
[40] Ah! the strange splendor

The fir-trees shall know!
And so,
Little evergreens, grow!
Grow, grow!
Grow, little evergreens, grow!

[41]

THE WREN-HOUSE

Yesterday I took my saw
And some bits of wood,
And I made a little house
Nicely as I could.

I put on a mossy-green
Little pointed roof,
And I cut a tiny door
That is pussy-proof.

For I hope some little wrens
To our yard will come
And will choose my little house
For their little home.

I shall hang it in the boughs
Of the apple-tree,
And I'm sure as rent for it
They will sing to me!

[42]

THE BABY'S RIDE

Chee! Chee! Chickadee!
Sing-time and sun!

Aye, aye, baby-bye,
Springtime has begun!

In the little willow cart,
On a downy bed,
Pretty parasol of silk
Swinging overhead,

Let us go along the lane
Where a baby sees
Mighty tufts of grass, and weeds
Tall as forest trees!
[43]
Bluebird on the apple-bough,
Sing and sing and sing!
Sing your very sweetest now
For babyhood and spring!

"Bah! Bah!" from the pasture,
And "Caw! Caw!" from the crow,
And bleating from the little calf
That has not learned to low.

Apple-buds, apple-buds breaking apart,
The baby looks upward with love-laden gaze;
Oh, shower some petals down here in his cart,
One honey-sweet cluster of pretty pink sprays!
[44]
Apple-buds, apple-buds, scornful and too
Vain of your loveliness, stay where you are!
The cheeks of the baby are pinker than you,
And finer and softer and sweeter by far!

See the pretty little lambs,
How they frisk and play!
See their silky fleeces shine
White as buds in May!

White as are the fleecy clouds
Softly blowing by—
What if they were little lambs
Playing in the sky?

Robin on the peach-bough,
Swinging overhead,
Sing a little song and say
Why is your breast so red?
[45]
Why is your voice so sweet, and
Your song so merry, say?
And wherefore do you spread your wings
And quickly fly away?

Ho, ho! see the queer little prints there
That cover the road, baby, look!
At the web-footed tangle that hints where
The ducks have gone down to the brook!

The Muscovy mammas that waddled
Zigzag, you can trace in their tracks,
And the dear little ducklings that toddled
And tumbled sometimes on their backs!

Buttercup, buttercup, buttercup gold,
O give us a handful of riches to hold!
[46]

Ho, ho! laughs the baby, and grasps in his glee
His wealth, but soon shows what a spend-thrift is he!
—Nay, nay, he is king, though he never was crowned,
And royally scatters his gold on the ground!

Bough of the willow-tree
Over the brook,
Down darts a kingfisher,
Look, baby, look!

Back on the willow-bough,
Fishing is done;
Happy and nappy now
There in the sun.

[47] Happy and nappy the baby is, too,
Softly his eyelids droop over the blue,
Golden his curls on the white pillow lie,
Sleep, baby, sleep, baby, hush-a-by-bye.

[48]

AN INDIAN RAID

Did you see some Indians passing,
Just a short while back?
Looks as if they must be massing
For a fierce attack!

Buckskin fringes, turkey-feather
Huge head-dresses and
Bows and arrows, altogether

Quite a frightful band!

From the lilac-bushes springing,
See them rushing! Ugh!
Awful war-whoops wildly ringing!
There'll be scalping, too!

In their fearful frenzy leaping,
It is very plain
Soon around us they'll be heaping
Mountains of the slain!
[49]
Soon their victims will be falling—
But, above the noise,
Hark! I hear somebody calling,
"Come to dinner, boys!"

[50]

THE FIRST SLEIGH-RIDE

O happy time of fleecy rime
And falling flakes, and O
The glad surprise in baby eyes
That never saw the snow!

Down shining ways the flying sleighs
Go jingling by, and see!
Beside the gate the horses wait
And neigh for you and me!

[51]

SLEEPY TIME

Hey, baby! Ho, baby! here upon my knee,
See the firelight flicker over you and me!

See the tiny people basking in the glow,
Peering through the ruddy little coals, and so

How they dance and scamper! Merry fairy folk!
Little sparks for spangles, little wings of smoke!

Come baby, come baby, nestle in my arms;
Hear the purring flames now sing their sleepy charms.

All the firelight fairies, all the drowsy elves,
In the downy ashes cover up themselves.

And I fold the little blanket over you;
Bye baby, my baby, let us slumber too.

[52]

WHEN BETTIE AND ANNE WENT WALKING

When they took their dollies walking,
They were both so busy talking,
(They had not met for half an hour and so had much to say)
That they heedlessly kept going
Down the shady streets, not knowing,
Till they wanted to come back again, they could not find the way!

In their fright they felt forlorner
Every time they turned a corner,
And they wailed to one another, "Oh, whatever shall we do?
A big bear might come to bite us,
Or a dreadful dog to fight us,

Or the wicked gipsies get us! *Oh, boo-hoo! Boo-hoo! Boo-hoo!*"
[53]
But this story, though a sad one,
Has an end that's not a bad one,
For at last somebody found them as they bade the world good-by;
They took their dollies home again,
And vowed they'd never roam again,
And their mothers hugged and kissed them, saying, "There, my dears, don't cry!"

[54]

THE BLUEBIRD

To-day at dawn there twinkled through
The pearly mist a flash of blue
So dazzling bright I thought the sky
Shone through the rifted clouds on high,
Till, by and by,
A note so honey-sweet I heard,
I knew that bright flash was a bird!

[55]

THE ORGAN-GRINDER

Hark! I hear the organ-grinder
Coming down the street,
And the sudden clatter-patter
Of the children's feet!

Come, oh, let us run to meet him!
Did you ever hear
Tunes so gay as he is playing,

Or so sweet and clear?

See the brown-faced little monkey,
Impudent and bold,
With his little scarlet jacket
Braided all in gold!

And his tiny cap and tassel
Bobbing to and fro,
Look, oh, look! he plucks it off now,
Bowing very low.
[56]
And he's passing it politely—
Can it be for *pay*?
O dear me! I have no penny!
Let us run away!

[57]

THE NEW MOON

Pretty new moon, little new moon,
Now, as first I look at you,
I must make a wish, for wise folks
Say it surely will come true!

Little new moon, pretty new moon,
I wish—but I must not tell!
For if any one should hear it,
Wise folks say it breaks the spell!

[58]

SHOWERY TIME

The April rain-drops tinkle
In cuckoo-cups of gold,
And warm south winds unwrinkle
The buds the peach-boughs hold.

In countless fluted creases
The little elm-leaves show,
While white as carded fleeces
The dogwood blossoms blow.

A rosy robe is wrapping
The early red-bud trees;
But still the haws are napping,
Nor heed the honey-bees.

And still in lazy sleeping
The apple-buds are bound,
But tulip-tips are peeping
From out the garden ground.
[59]
And yonder, gayly swinging
Upon the turning vane,
A robin redbreast singing
Makes merry at the rain!

[60]

EASTER DAY

Christ the Lord is risen to-day!
Angels rolled the stone away
From the tomb wherein He lay!

Little children, come and sing,
"Glory, glory to the King,

Christ the Lord of everything!"

[61]

THE SANDMAN

The Sandman! hark, I hear him!
He's coming up the stair,
And everybody near him
Is nodding, I declare!

He's peeping in the door now,
And first of all he spies,
As he has done before now,
The little children's eyes!

Then quickly does he throw it,
His golden sleepy-sand,
And all, before they know it,
Are off for sleepy-land!

[62]

DANDELION CURLS

Ah, ha, ha, now! who comes here
Wreathed in flowers of gold and queer
Tiny tangled curls of green
Gayly bobbing in between?

Pretty token of the spring!
Hark! we hear the bluebirds sing
When we thus see little girls
Decked in dandelion curls.

[63]

POP-CORN

Pop! Pop! – Poppetty-pop!
Shake and rattle and rattle and shake
The golden grains as they bounce and break
To fluffy puffiness—*Poppetty-pop!*
Bursting and banging the popper's top!
Poppetty-pop!
Pop! Pop!
The yellow kernels, oh, see them grow
White as cotton or flakes of snow!
Pop! Pop!
O-ho, how they frolic and fly about
And turn themselves suddenly inside out!
Pop-pop-poppetty! Pop-pop-pop!
The popper's full and we'll have to stop;
Pile the bowl with the tempting treat,
Children, come, it is time to eat!

[64]

THE RASH LITTLE SPARROW

Rash little sparrow
Up in the nest;
Feathers not long enough,
Wee wings not strong enough!
Poor little sparrow!
Poor little breast!

[65]

WHAT IF?

When I see the new moon lightly
Through cloud ripples slip,
Then I'm sure that shining brightly
It's a fairy ship!

What if in it we were sailing
Far and far away,
With a wake of silver trailing,
Till the golden day?

Why, we'd fly back home together
Safely from the sky,
For the moon's a fairy feather
When the sun is high!

[66]

EASTER EGGS

Seven little nests of hay
We have made, for Easter day
Is to-morrow, and you know
We must have them ready, so
When the Rabbit comes she'll see
We expected her, that we
Children tried our very best
Each to make the nicest nest.

One is in the lilac-bush,
Near the ground—last year a thrush
Built a nest there—let me see,
Two are by the apple-tree,
In the clover—that makes three—
One beside the playhouse door,
—Three plus one, that must be four—
[67] Two are in the tulip-bed—

Was it seven that I said?
Oh, yes! six I've counted, and
One is in our pile of sand.

Come and see! Oh, hurry, hurry!
For the Rabbit, kind and furry,
Has been here again and laid
Eggs in every nest we made!
Purple, orange, red, and blue,
Pink and green and yellow, too,
Like a bunch of finest flowers
Ever seen, and all are ours!
And oh, *look!* What *do* you think!
Here our names are in white ink,
All spelled nicely so we know
Just where every egg should go!
Is it not surprising, quite,
How well Easter Rabbits write?

[68]

THE BIRDS' BATH

In our garden we have made
Such a pretty little pool,
Lined with pebbles neatly laid,
Filled with water clean and cool.

THE BIRDS' BATH

When the sun shines warm and high
Robins cluster round its brink,
Never one comes flying by

But will flutter down to drink.

Then they splash and splash and splash,
Spattering little showers bright
All around, till off they flash
Singing sweetly their delight.

[69]

NOVEMBER MORNING

A tingling, misty marvel
Blew hither in the night,
And now the little peach-trees
Are clasped in frozen light.

Upon the apple-branches
An icy film is caught,
With trailing threads of gossamer
In pearly patterns wrought.

The autumn sun, in wonder,
Is gayly peering through
This silver-tissued network
Across the frosty blue.

The weather-vane is fire-tipped,
The honeysuckle shows
A dazzling icy splendor,
And crystal is the rose.
[70]
Around the eaves are fringes
Of icicles that seem
To mock the summer rainbows
With many-colored gleam.

Along the walk, the pebbles
Are each a precious stone;
The grass is tasseled hoarfrost,
The clover jewel-sown.

Such sparkle, sparkle, sparkle
Fills all the frosty air,
Oh, can it be that darkness
Is ever anywhere!

[71]

THE RUNAWAY

A frantic clatter of horses' feet!
A runaway's coming down the street!
Flurry, scurry,
Children, hurry!
Drop your playthings! Quick! don't wait!
Run and get within the gate!
Push the baby in the door,
Scramble in yourselves before
—*Whoa! Whoa!*
There they go!
Pell-mell rushing, snorting, quaking,
Wagon rumbling, harness breaking,
Frightened so they cannot know
Everybody's shrieking "*Whoa!*"
O my, don't cry!
Whiz, bang, they've galloped by!
[72] No one hurt, but horses dashed
Round a post and wagon smashed!
Dear me! Dear me!
When a runaway we see,
Children, too, must run, oh, fast!
Run and hide as it goes past!

[73]

LOST!

"Peep! Peep! Peep!" Poor little chick!
Little cry so weak and small,
Meadow grass so tall and thick,
And the clover tufts so tall!

Little heart in sore distress,
Longing for the mother wing;
Through the weedy wilderness
Searching for its sheltering!

[74]

THE QUEEN'S PAGE

Once I was a little page
To a May-day queen,
And I wore a little coat
Made of Lincoln green.

Oh, the queen was beautiful!
And she had a bright
Crown of golden cuckoo-buds
And violets blue and white.

On the step beside her throne
I sat very still,
Ready, as a page should be,
To obey her will.

And before us little girls,
Each with garlands gay,
Round a May-pole danced and sang
Almost all the day.

[75]

OUR TREE-TOAD

Grandfather says the tree-toad,
That to our yard has come,
Is just a little wee toad
No bigger than his thumb!

And that his coat's so queer it
Can turn from green to blue!
Whatever color's near it,
Why, that's its color, too!

And then Grandfather snickers
And says, "Would you suppose
He climbs with little stickers
On all his little toes?

"And don't you wish your toes now
Were fixed like his? For, see,
Right up the elm he goes now
And sticks tight to the tree!"
[76]
"But then," he says, "O dear me!
If all the little boys
Could *screech* as loud, I fear me
There'd be a dreadful noise!"

[77]

IN THE WATER-WORLD

Down among the water-weeds,
Darting through the grass,
Round about the tasseled reeds,
See the minnows pass!
See the little turtles there,

Hiding, half asleep,
Tucked in tangled mosses where
Tiny crayfish creep!

Watch the trailing grasses string
Strands of purple shells
That the lazy ripples ring,
Sweet as silver bells;
Watch the sunshine sift and drift
Down the eddy whirls,
Whence the laden whiteweeds lift
Loads of blossom pearls;
[78]
While the limpid shadows slip
Softly in between,
And the pussy-willows dip
Lightly in the green
Of the mocking trees that grow
Down the water-sky,
Flecked with fleecy clouds that blow
Where the reed-birds fly.

Oh, such marvels manifold
Fill the summer stream,
Such enticing things untold
Through the ripples gleam,
If you could a moment turn
Into what you wish,
Would it not be fun to be
Yonder little fish?

[79]

WHO WAS IT?

Of course I've heard the moon's green cheese,
But will somebody tell me, please,

Who was it took so big a bite
There's scarcely any left to-night?

[80]

VISITING DAY

I'll wear the striped skirt that trails,
And you the flowered one,
And we will take our parasols
And walk out in the sun.

We'll leave our dolly-carts at home,
For ladies, when they call,
Must not have children with them, no,
That would not do at all.

And I'll be "Mrs. Wilkinson,"
And you'll be "Mrs. Brown,"
And we will call and call and call
On every one in town!

[81]

A VALENTINE TO CATHERINE

If you will be my True-Love,
I'll tell you what I'll do,
I'll ask a little bluebird
To sing a song to you.

When first you see a violet
And softly pricking through
The garden-bed come crocuses
And golden tulips, too,

Then watch! for he'll be coming,
The little bird of blue;
He'll sing, "I love you, Sweetheart,
It's true, true, true!"

[82]

FIREFLIES

Look! Look down in the garden how
The firefly lights are flitting now!
A million tiny sparks I know
Flash through the pinks and golden-glow,
And I am very sure that all
Have come to light a fairy ball,
And if I could stay up I'd see
How gay the fairy folks can be!

[83]

THE RAINY DAY

Let's sail all day, away, away
To the splendid Spanish Main
And the sultry seas of the Caribbees
And skies that never rain!

As pirates bold with bags of gold
And cutlasses and things,
We'll pack doubloons and silver spoons
In chests with iron rings.

And these we'll carry and secretly bury
In cannibal isles afar;
Like Captain Kidd, when they're safely hid

We won't tell where they are.

Let's sail all day, away, away
To the splendid Spanish Main
And the sultry seas of the Caribbees
—But at night sail home again!

[84]

THE FIRST RED-BIRD

I heard a song at daybreak,
So honey-sweet and clear,
The essence of all joyous things
Seemed mingling in its cheer.

The frosty world about me
I searched with eager gaze,
But all was slumber-bound and wrapped
In violet-tinted haze.

Then suddenly a sunbeam
Shot slanting o'er the hill,
And once again from out the sky
I heard that honied trill.
[85]
And there upon a poplar,
Poised at its topmost height,
I saw a little singer clad
In scarlet plumage bright.

The poplar branches quivered,
By dawn winds lightly blown,
And like a breeze-swept poppy-flower
The red-bird rocked and shone.

The blue sky, and his feathers
Flashed o'er by golden light,
Oh, all my heart with rapture thrilled,
It was so sweet a sight!

[86]

THE WEATHER-VANE

Turn, turn, when pelting rain
Rushes down the window-pane;
Turn, turn, and turn again
When the sun shines, weather-vane!

Fie! Fie! to always be
Emblem of uncertainty!
Followed by the restless sea,
Changeful moons may wax and wane,
Yet the moons and sea-tides, too,
Constant are compared to you!
Fickle still you must remain
Long as winds blow, weather-vane!

[87]

THE SWAN

Stately swan, so proud and white
Glistening in the morning light,
Come and tell me is it true
That a snow-white swan like you,
Guided by bright golden chains
In his beak for bridle reins,
Once upon a time from far
Fabled lands where fairies are
Brought a magic boat wherein

Rode the brave knight Lohengrin?

Stately swan, so proud and white
Glistening in the morning light,
If you only wore a gold
Harness, like that swan of old,
And if trailing in your wake
Sailing on the silver lake
[88] Was a boat of magic and
You could float to fairy-land,
Then I'd jump in and begin
Traveling like Lohengrin!

[89]

BABY'S BAKING

So, so, spade and hoe,
Little pile of sand;
See it turning into dough
In the baby's hand!

Little pie with crimpy crust,
Set it in the sun;
Sugar it with powdered dust,
And bake it till it's done.

[90]

A SURE SIGN

When you see upon the walk
Circles newly made of chalk,
And around them all the day
Little boys in eager play
Rolling marbles, agates fine,

Banded, polished, red as wine,
Marbles crystal as the dew,
Each with rainbows twisted through,
Marbles gay in painted clay,
Flashing, twinkling in your way,
When the walk has blossomed so,
Surely every one must know
None need wonder who has heard
Robin, wren, or Peter-bird;
Sure the sign as song or wing,
It is spring!

[91]

ANOTHER SURE SIGN

When pink-cheeked on every hand
Little girls are seen to stand
Turning skipping ropes,—*swish-swash!*—
While their laughing playmates run
Jumping over,—oh, what fun!—
Swish-swash! Swish-swash!
Two and two now, see them dash!
One, two, one, two,
Round they scamper, safely through,
Swish-swash! such merry skipping,
One, two,—some one is tripping!
Ah, she's out now and must pay
Turning rope while others play!
See the bobbing golden curls,
Little skirts in rhythmic swirls
[92] Rising, falling, to the beat
Of the little skipping feet!
When these pretty sights appear,
It is surely very clear
April's here!

[93]

THE ROBIN'S BATH

A flash and flicker of dripping wings,
A wet red breast that glows
Bright as the newly opened bud
The first red poppy shows,
A sparkle of flying rainbow drops,
A glint of golden sun
On ruffled feathers, a snatch of song,
And the robin's bath is done.

[94]

THE FROSTED PANE

When I wakened, very early,
All my window-pane was pearly
With a sparkling little picture traced in lines of shining white;
Some magician with a gleaming
Frosty brush, while I was dreaming,
Must have come and by the starlight worked through all the quiet night.

He had painted frosty people,
And a frosty church and steeple,
And a frosty bridge and river tumbling over frosty rocks;
Frosty mountain peaks that glimmered,
And fine frosty ferns that shimmered,
And a frosty little pasture full of frosty little flocks.
[95]
It was all touched in so lightly
And it glittered, oh, so whitely,
That I gazed and gazed in wonder at the lovely painted pane;
Then the sun rose high and higher

With his wand of golden fire
Till, alas, my picture vanished and I looked for it in vain!

[96]

THE FIRST SNOW

The snow! the snow! Whoop! Hooray! Ho! Ho!
Plunge in the deep drifts and toss it up so!
Rollick and roll in the feathery fleece
Plucked out of the breasts of the marvelous geese
By the little old woman who lives in the sky;
Have ever you seen her? No, neither have I!

[97]

GRANDFATHER KNOWS

Grandfather says of all things
The silliest he's heard
Is that some children call things
They've never seen, "absurd!"
And have their doubts of true things,
And won't believe, because
They say, "If you but knew things,
There *is* no Santa Claus!"

Grandfather says he *knows* him,
And sees him every year,
And Santa often shows him
The playthings he brings here;
He says, too, Santa told him
If any girls and boys
Laugh at and won't uphold him,
They'll not get any toys!

[98]

SLEIGH-BELLS

Tinkle, tinkle, tinkle!
Happy winter-time!
Baby's eyes a-twinkle,
Hear the sleigh-bells chime!

Each one rings a merry
Ting-a-ling-a-ling!
For a sleigh-bell fairy
Hides inside to sing.

See them quake and quiver,
Up and downward tossed,
Seems as if they shiver
In the nipping frost!

Shiver into laughter,
Jolly little elves!
Till we laugh thereafter,
Merry as themselves!

[99]

THE RED-BIRD

Swept lightly by the south wind
The elm-leaves softly stirred,
And in their pale green clusters
There straightway bloomed a bird!

His glossy feathers glistened
With dyes as richly red
As any tulip flaming
From out the garden bed.

But ah, unlike the tulips,
In joyous strain, ere long,
This red-bird flower unfolded
A heart of golden song!

[100]

WILD BEASTS

I will be a lion
And you shall be a bear,
And each of us will have a den
Beneath a nursery chair;
And you must growl and growl and growl,
And I will roar and roar,
And then—why, then—you'll growl again,
And I will roar some more!

[101]

WHEREFORE WINGS?

Heigho, sparrow! Reckless of the rain;
When chill the cheerless wind grows,
Chirping might and main!
Is it naught, then, when the rose
Blows again?

Beating, sleeting on your draggled coat!
Surely, 'tis enough to drown
Any happy note
Nestling in that downy brown
Little throat.

Ah me, sparrow! Had I but your power,
Think you in the freezing sleet

I would waste an hour?
—I'd sing my sweetest to a sweet
Orange flower!

[102]

BASKING

Frosty winter chased away
By the blessed sun,
Down upon the garden walks
Basking has begun.

Oh, the happy, happy heat!
How the pulses stir,
How it warms the hearts beneath
Little coats of fur!

Oh, the happy pussy-cats!
Days to doze and doze,
And what pleasant dreams they dream
Only pussy knows.

[103]

WITH A MAY-BASKET FOR BABY AGNES

Peach-buds to meet thee,
Robins to greet thee,
Hey, little Sweetheart! and May morning, hey!
Sunbeam and sing time,
Bluebird and wing time,
This time is kiss time for sweethearts, I say!

Dearest, God bless thee,
Fold and caress thee,

Unto thy cradle may good fairies fly!
Fortune be fair for thee,
This is my prayer for thee,
Lullaby, little one, hush-a-by-bye!
[104]
So for a love now
Token thereof now,
Sweet, see this tiny May-basket I bring;
Posies to play with,
Pinks to be gay with,
Dear little baby of sunshine and spring!

[105]

THE LITTLE NEST

A little picture haunts me;
It comes and comes again;
It is a tiny bird's-nest,
All ragged from the rain.

It clings within a birch-tree
Upon the moorland's edge,
Between the barren branches,
Above the swaying sedge.

The sky is gray behind it,
And when the north winds blow,
The birch-tree bends and shivers,
And tosses to and fro.

I wonder, does it haunt them,
The birds that flew away?
And will they come to seek it,
Some sunny summer day?
[106]

I wonder, does some redbreast
Upon an orange-bough,
Still picture it as plainly
As I can see it now?

Ah me! I would forget it,
Yet still, with sense of pain,
I see this little bird's-nest
Within the driving rain.

[107]

CHRISTMAS CANDLES

When the Christ-child comes again
Softly down the street to-night,
Twinkling through the window pane
Let our candles shed their light.

Though the clouds are dark above
And the golden stars are dim,
We can tell Him of our love
If we set a light for Him.

Oh, the blessed Christ-child dear,
In His robe of shining white,
Let our candles give Him cheer
As He passes by to-night!

[108]

A SONG OF THE CHRISTMAS-TREE

CHRISTMAS CANDLES

We can tell Him of our love
If we set a light for Him.

Hurrah! Hurrah! for the Christmas-tree
With its glory and glitter and mystery!
Its twinkling candles that bud and bloom
Like strange bright flowers in the darkened room,
Its glistening gold and silver balls,
Its candy canes and its blue-eyed dolls,
The sugary fruits it bears,—for oh,
Where else do such wonderful sweetmeats grow?—
Its tasseled horns and its pop-corn strings
And all its myriad marvelous things!
O-ho! and ah-ha!
And a hip hurrah!
For our dear and beautiful tree, because
It grew in the gardens of Santa Claus
[109]
And he brought it here in his reindeer sleigh
From ever and ever so far away!
So, children, come, let us make a ring
And all clasp hands as we dance and sing
To the blessed tree and the blessed night
When the Christ-child walks in the candles' light!

Hurrah! Hurrah! for the Christmas-tree
That Santa Claus brought to you and me!
He cut it down with a silver axe—
There's a tree in each of his million packs!—
And carried it safely over the snow
And down our chimney and here, you know;
Its golden cobwebs that glint and gleam
He took from a lovely Christmas dream
And tangled them over it till, behold,
It shines like the fabled Fleece of Gold!
[110]

Oh, Santa Claus, here's
A thrice three cheers
For garlands green and berries of red,
And mistletoe clustering overhead,
For the joy of our Christmas festival!
But our beautiful tree, it is best of all!
And circling still in a merry ring
We'll still clasp hands as we dance and sing
To the blessed tree and the blessed night
When the Christ-child walks in the candles' light!

Hurrah! Hurrah! for the Christmas-tree!
And look, O look to its tip and see
The feathery slim fir leaves and where,
In the topmost boughs, is the image fair
Of the Christ-child nestling amid the green
And the little brown cones that peep between!
[111]
And high above Him glittering bright
A gold star sparkles with golden light,
And we children think, as we gaze on them,
Of the wonderful Star of Bethlehem,
Of the lovely Star
And the Kings who far,
Oh, far, came seeking a Babe and brought
Their love and worship to Him they sought,
And made Him gifts, as the gifts we make
With loving hearts for that Baby's sake.
Oh, come, come all, and join the ring!
Let all clasp hands as we dance and sing
To the blessed tree and the blessed night
When the Christ-child walks in the candles' light!

[112]

OUR KITTENS

Our kittens have the softest fur,
And the sweetest little purr,
And such little velvet paws
With such cunning little claws,
And blue eyes, just like the sky!
(*Must* they turn green, by and by?)
Two are striped like tigers, three
Are as black as black can be,
And they run so fast and play
With their tails, and are so gay,
Is it not a pity that
Each must grow into a cat?

[113]

IN JULY

Let us find a shady wady
Pretty little brook;
Let us have some candy handy,
And a picture-book.

There all day we'll stay and play and
Never mind the heat,
While the water gleaming, streaming,
Ripples round our feet.

And we'll gather curly pearly
Mussel-shells while bright
Frightened minnows darting, parting,
Scurry out of sight.

What if, what if,—heigho! my oh!—
All the "ifs" were true,
And the little fishes wishes,

Now, what would you do?

[114]

A VALENTINE TO A LITTLE CHILD

Dear heart, on this thrice-blessed day,
An thou my sweetheart be,
The rose of love shall bide alway
Upon the red-rose tree.

And in the garden of my heart
So ceaselessly shall shine,
The little birds will know thou art
Mine own true Valentine.

And I will bid them wing and sing
To all good winds that blow,
That to thy little feet they bring
All blessings, even so.

And o'er thy cradle I will coax,
By every lucky charm,
The friendship of the fairy folks
To fold thee from all harm.
[115]
So may they hover round thy head
And gently thereupon,
As doth the April sunshine, shed
Most gracious benison.

And all fair gifts that Fortune hath,
I'll pray she promise these,
And that she loose about thy path
All sweet influences.

Then here's a kiss! and there's a kiss!
And kisses, one, two, three!
I seal them in the folds of this,
And speed them unto thee!

[116]

ZIP!

When we went to drive the cows home
Down the lane to-day,
There was such a funny bunny
Jumped across the way!

All we saw as he ran past us,
Faster than a quail,
Was his snow-white fuzzy-wuzzy
Little cotton tail!

[117]

A LITTLE CAROL

Welcome, little Brother!
Lowly, holy One!
Hail thee, Virgin Mother,
More than any other
Blessed in thy Son!

Child, since the poor manger
Once thou didst not scorn,
Rest thee, little Stranger,
Folded from all danger,
In our hearts new-born!

Nestle thus, we pray thee,
In our love's caress;
Fain we are to pay thee
Worship, and obey thee,
Babe, and Prince no less!

[118]

SONG

Honey-dew drippity-drops for a feast,
Dreams of delight when the feasting has ceased,
Poppy and rose,
Drain them and doze;
This is a song that the butterfly knows.

[119]

THE THREE CANDLES

When the Christmas-tide drew nigh,
On a shelf three candles bright,
Two were red and one was white,
Waited for who came to buy.

Said the first one, "I shall be
Chosen for a Christmas-tree!"
Said the second, "I shall light
Christ Jesus on His way to-night!"
Then the third one sighed, "Ah me,
I know not what my lot will be!"

When the dark fell, bright and gay
The first candle burned away,
Red as all the berries red
On the holly overhead,

While the children in their glee
Danced around the Christmas-tree.
[120]
And the second, twinkling bright,
Poured forth all its golden light
Through a window decked with green
Garlands and red ribbons' sheen,
So the Christ-child when He came
Might be guided by its flame.

But the third one in the gloom
Of a bare and cheerless room
Softly burned where long had lain
A poor little child in pain,
And the baby in its bed
By the light was comforted.

When the Christ-child passed that night
All three candles gave Him light,
But the brightest was the spark
By the baby in the dark.

THE END